MW00945249

Other Dover Books by
ANNA STAROBINETS

In the Wolf's Lair

Claws of Rage

The Plucker

A Predator's Rights
A BEASTLY CRIMES BOOK

BOOK 2

ANNA STAROBINETS

Translated by
Jane Bugaeva

Illustrated by
Marie Muravski

Dover Publications, Inc.
Mineola, New York

Bibliographical Note

This Dover edition, first published in 2019, is an unabridged English translation of the Russian work originally printed by Clever, Moscow, Russia, in 2016.

Library of Congress Cataloging-in-Publication Data

Names: Starobineëtis, Anna, author. | Muravski, Marie, illustrator. | Bugaeva, Jane, translator.
Title: A predator's rights : a Beastly crimes book / Anna Starobinets ; translated by Jane Bugaeva ; illustrated by Marie Muravski.
Other titles: Pravo khishchnika. English
Description: Mineola, New York : Dover Publications, 2019. | Series: Beastly crimes ; book 2 | "This Dover edition, first published in 2019, is a translation of an unabridged republication of the work originally printed by Clever, Moscow, Russia, in 2016." | Summary: Chief Badger and Badgercat investigate when a missing chicken, destined for the soup pot, disappears from Huntington Farm, causing the guard dogs to start a Hunt in the Near Woods.
Identifiers: LCCN 2018029284| ISBN 9780486829517 (hardback) | ISBN 0486829510
Subjects: | CYAC: Criminal investigation—Fiction. | Murder—Fiction. | Badgers—Fiction. | Chickens—Fiction. | Dogs—Fiction. | Forest animals—Fiction. | Mystery and detective stories. | BISAC: JUVENILE FICTION / Animals / Dogs. | JUVENILE FICTION/ Animals / Farm Animals. | JUVENILE FICTION / Humorous Stories.
Classification: LCC PZ7.1.S738 Pre 2019 | DDC [Fic]—dc23
LC record available at https://lccn.loc.gov/2018029284

Manufactured in the United States by LSC Communications
82951001   2019
www.doverpublications.com

CONTENTS

CONTENTS

A Predator's Rights

CHAPTER I: IN WHICH EVERYTHING IS DONE TO SAVE THE VICTIM

"**S**he's not breathing," said Doc Hawk. "I'll try beak to beak resuscitation. It's a long shot, but I'll fight for her life with everything I've got."

Doc Hawk turned away, spread his wings, inhaled deeply, and began fighting for her life. He pressed his curved, steel-gray beak against her pointed, yellow, lifeless one. For a few seconds the only sound was Hawk's rhythmic breathing—inhale, exhale, inhale, exhale... The victim didn't move. She was lying on a soft, snow-white rug made of poplar fluff, her neck twisted at an unnatural angle. Her eyes were glazed over, staring blindly at the ceiling intricately lined with oblong black river stones and the red petals of wild roses.

After another minute, when they'd all but lost hope, she suddenly stirred and they heard a hoarse, muffled clucking.

"Who am I? Where am I?" whispered the chicken. "Is this a cloud? Is this heaven?"

"She's alive," exhaled Chief Badger, relieved, having watched the whole ordeal. He turned to the chicken, "This isn't a cloud. This is Fox's den. I'm so happy you're alive."

"Who am I? Where am I?" repeated the chicken, overtaken by a fit of coughing.

"Chickens are very resilient," Badgercat spoke up. "And stupid. I heard you can bite their head off and they'll still run around for a while, because they don't understand that they don't have a head anymore..."

"I ought to bite your head off for such anecdotes," said Hawk. "Yours, too," he turned to Fox, "for almost killing her. Chickens are frail, vulnerable animals. Their lives are priceless! But so easy to take! In fact, the situation was quite hopeless—"

"Where's my head?" The chicken rose and, swaying, took a couple of steps on the poplar fluff rug.

"You shouldn't be up!" squawked Hawk. "You're still very weak. In fact, the situation was quite hopeless! I always fight to the end, always perform beak to beak—"

"Thank you, Doctor," said Chief Badger. "This chicken is alive, thanks to you."

"This chicken is alive, thanks to my weak jaw," protested Fox. "And it's weak because I only eat vegetables, even though I'm a predator... Oh dear! She's ruining my rug!"

"Predatory vegetables," trilled the chicken, her pace quickening.

"Be careful—that's custom spun!" squealed Fox, but it was too late. The chicken had wobbled over to the window and rammed her beak into a superfine cobweb curtain, causing the silvery threads to strain and tear. The chicken, all wrapped up in the curtain and its alder catkin tassels, began flapping her wings wildly, knocking over a vase that held a bouquet of juniper branches and maple leaves.

"I should've worked on strengthening my jaw muscles...," whispered Fox.

"You don't seem to feel any guilt," Chief Badger's whiskers stiffened indignantly.

"It's easy to place blame on a helpless, fluffy fox." Fox fluttered her ginger eyelashes, and her chin began to quiver. "But what—what am I guilty of?"

"Of attacking a peaceful animal. And of attempted murder."

"Animal?" Fox grew pale. "What are you talking about? I didn't attack any animals! Just a chicken."

"Attack," said the chicken, floundering in the curtain.

"And what, a chicken isn't an animal?" asked Badger, amazed.

"Of course not! We—you and I—we're animals. Animals live in the woods. Animals are wild. The law of the Far Woods says that wild animals cannot eat one another. But chickens are domestic birds. They aren't animals, they're game. Predators have the right to—"

"But that's..." Hawk's voice trembled. "That's so beastly! That's clear-cut game-ism! Separating animals into wild and domestic, into animals and nonanimals! That kind of thinking could be used to justify anything—like saying that all birds, domestic or not, are game! And predators have the right to..." Hawk gulped. "All animal lives are priceless! Why are the police turning a blind eye to this?"

Badgercat looked down and began thoroughly examining the claws on his right front paw.

"Game-ism is unacceptable," said Chief Badger sternly. "Predators do not have the right to kill chickens."

"Kill," said the chicken, shutting her eyes tightly.

"But there's nothing about chickens in the laws of the Far Woods," protested Fox.

"But there is something about chickens in the laws of Huntington Farm," said Badger. "It says that theft of rural livestock and poultry by a resident of the Far Woods is punishable by the mauling of that resident!"

"Mauling?..." Fox grew pale.

"Mauling," said the chicken.

"...and if the authorities of the Far Woods do not turn over the perpetrator, then Huntington Farm sends a pack of hunting dogs to the woods," continued Badger. "A Hunt—that's what's in our future if we don't turn you over to the farm. Do you understand, Fox? Do you understand what you've gotten us into?"

"So you're...going to give me up...to be mauled?" Fox began shaking. "A helpless, fluffy fox? Who had no idea...didn't expect...and besides, she was given permission to kill the chicken...by a police officer!" Fox began sobbing.

"Kill the chicken, kill the chicken, kill the chicken...," clucked the chicken.

"A police officer?" Badger frowned. "Who are you talking about, Fox?"

Badgercat flicked his tail nervously from side to side.

"...kill the chicken, kill the chicken, kill the chicken!"

"The patient is hysterical," said Hawk.

"Then do something to calm her down, doctor!" said Badger, annoyed.

"Please take this soothing sedative," said Hawk, slighted. He dug around in his bag, producing a large Hawthorn berry. He put it in the chicken's beak.

Chief Badger looked at Fox, then at Badgercat.

"Which police officer are you talking about, Fox?"

"This one," sniffled Fox, pointing at Badgercat. "He said I could."

"You really gave her permission to kill a chicken, Badgercat?" Badger slumped in disappointment, suddenly looking very small. "When you said that to the head guard dog, I thought you were just protecting Fox. But you really did...?"

"I thought...I just wanted to..." Badgercat closed his eyes. "Fox promised to give an eyewitness account in return for the right to kill...just one...farm chicken... I thought it wouldn't be a big deal..."

"I need some fresh air," said the chicken and promptly fell asleep.

"What have you done, Badgercat?" said Chief Badger, crestfallen. "It's one thing if Fox, without thinking, succumbed to her predatory instincts and committed the crime. Then all the fault would be on her. We could've worked something out with Huntington Farm. But it's another thing if her crime was permitted by the police of the Far Woods—as if attacking farm animals is normal to us. To all of us. Now Huntington Farm will consider all residents of the Far Woods dangerous. How could you? You've provoked a Hunt! There'll be bloodshed! A beastly massacre."

"If I may," Hawk cut in politely. "I'm categorically against a Hunt. We must avoid bloodshed! Maybe the fact that I was able to save the injured chicken will be of help in reaching an agreement with Huntington Farm?"

"I doubt it," Badger shook his head. "Muxtar said—"

"Who is Muxtar?" asked Fox fearfully.

"He's the head guard dog. He's some very unpleasant breed, maybe a boxer, or perhaps a wolfhound, or a cross between the two...Doctor, would you happen to have another sedative pill for the detained Fox? Anyway, Muxtar said it doesn't matter if the chicken is alive or not."

"Excuse me?" Hawk gaped. "What do you mean 'it doesn't matter'?"

"He said they were going to make soup out of the chicken, either way."

"What horror! How beastly!" Hawk glanced at the sleeping chicken, who looked like a swaddled newborn all wrapped up in the curtain. "Poor bird!"

"I know!" yelped Badgercat. "I know how to save the Far Woods from a Hunt! We need to get to the station!"

CHAPTER 2: IN WHICH A TRIUMPHANT ANTHEM IS SUNG

"**W**ould you like some more pine nuts?" Chief Badger politely asked the chicken. He was actually planning on feeding the pine nuts to Starling—who'd been confiscated from a criminal family of rabbits to serve the needs of the police department and who now lived at the station—but the chicken, upon seeing the food, had immediately flown up to the birdfeeder and gobbled up an entire portion. And then another. Now, with only one portion remaining, Badger hoped the chicken would tactfully decline.

"Would you like some more pine nuts?" said Starling in Badger's voice, glumly looking at the pile of nutshells. Starling had an amazing ability of mimicking voices, but the chicken wasn't the slightest bit impressed.

"I would," said the chicken and immediately gobbled up the last portion.

Absolutely no manners, thought Badger to himself. *This is what they call domesticated? In the Far Woods even the wildest animal is more courteous.*

"I hope you've remembered your name?" he asked out loud.

"No, I haven't. And I won't. I don't have a name."

"But...how should we address you?"

"I have a number," said the chicken proudly. "In our chicken coop everyone has a number. I'm Chicken Four. Return me to the coop."

"You like the coop?" asked Badgercat.

"I love it, and I'm proud of it."

"In our chicken coop everyone has a number," said Starling in the chicken's voice.

"Why do you love it?" asked Badgercat. "What are you proud of?"

"It's big and beautiful," said Chicken Four. "Everything is fair there. We are taken care of, we are fed, and we are protected."

"By whom?"

"Muxtar and the other guard dogs protect us. And Nina Palna takes care of us."

"What kind of animal is Nina Palna?"

"Nina Palna isn't an animal. She's a wonderful person. She loves chickens. But she's tough—the coop needs someone tough. She's kind but fair."

"Fair?" Badgercat narrowed his eyes. "Do you know what she does to chickens every Friday?"

"Every Friday she picks the best chicken in the coop and takes it to her kitchen," reported Chicken Four.

"So you know...," said Badgercat, shocked. "You know what happens to the chicken next?"

"A wonderful person. She loves chickens," said Starling in the chicken's voice.

"I know everything," said Chicken Four confidently. "In the kitchen, Nina Palna gives the best chicken a seat at the family's dinner table. She feeds her, pours her some tea, brushes her feathers, and then lays the chicken down to sleep in her own bed. All the best chickens stay to live with Nina Palna in her house."

"So that's the big lie," said Chief Badger thoughtfully.

"What do you mean—lie?" Chicken Four tensed up. "It's the truth."

"Every Friday, Nina Palna takes a chicken into the kitchen and chops off its head with a cleaver. And then she makes soup out of it!"

"Chops—what? With a—what?"

"Its head off. With a cleaver."

"And makes—what?"

"Soup. Chicken soup."

"Oh, you're joking," chortled Chicken Four.

"No, we're telling you the truth," said Badgercat seriously.

"Lies!" shrieked Chicken Four. "Foes of the coop! You're spreading lies about Nina Palna. And even if she wanted to make soup out of us, the loyal guard dogs would come to our rescue!"

"Nina Palna gives them the giblets and bones," said Badgercat. "If they came to your rescue they wouldn't get any dinner."

"Gib-b-b-lets?" Chicken Four choked out. "B-b-b-bones? Lies!"

"We have proof—a starling recording of our conversation with Muxtar," said Chief Badger. "One minute, I'll find it," he picked up Starling. "Rewind to this phrase: 'Dead or alive, I couldn't care less.'"

"Dead or alive, I couldn't care less," Starling growled menacingly in Muxtar's voice. "It's Chicken Fourrrrr—Nina Palna was planning on making soup out of her this Friday. So if you don't want a Hunt, return her to us in any condition. But we want the fox and kittyraccoon alive—live animals are always more fun to maul—"

"That's enough," interrupted Badgercat. "The rest isn't relevant."

For a minute Chicken Four stood silently, her beak agape. Her blood-red wattle trembled.

"The horror," she said finally. "And we lay eggs for her. Last week I gave Nina Palna all my eggs—every last one!" Her round eyes filled with tears. "And that's how she repays us? I don't want, don't want, don't want to be made into soup!" Chicken Four burst into tears.

"We can protect you," said Chief Badger. "If you agree to cooperate."

"Would you like me to lay you an egg?" she offered willingly.

"We don't need any eggs, thank you."

"But I can't lay anything else!" admitted Chicken Four.

"She's too dumb," Badgercat whispered in Badger's ear. "I'm afraid she won't be up to the task."

"Are you capable of memorizing a few lines?" Chief Badger asked the chicken.

"I'm the smartest chicken in our coop!" said Chicken Four proudly. "I've memorized all three stanzas of our anthem."

"How many stanzas did the dumbest chicken memorize?" asked Badgercat.

"None of the chickens in our coop are dumb," huffed Chicken Four. "Some are just less smart than others. The ones who are less smart can only memorize and repeat the first four words of our anthem: 'Hail to the coop!' Our anthem, by the way, is lovely. Listen," and she began singing:

Hail to the coop! Hail to the roosters!
Hail to the eggs and the hens!
We chickens are glorious nesters
Who lay again and again!

We chickens are the proudest breed
And spread our wings in awe
To celebrate heroic deeds
We proudly cluck hurrah!

O'er mountains and meadows
May we chickens keep soaring...

"Yes, may you keep soaring," interrupted Chief Badger. "Thank you for sharing, but that's enough.

We see that you have a very good memory. And you're very gifted. I'm sure you'll be able to help us."

"I'd like to finish our anthem," said Chicken Four stubbornly and started up again.

> O'er mountains and meadows
> May we chickens keep soaring!
> As we vanquish our foes
> 'All hail the coop,' we'll keep crowing!

CHAPTER 3: IN WHICH THERE'S A HUNTING HOUND

Meanwhile, back at the chicken coop: "Hail to the coop! Hail to the roosters! Hail to the eggs and the hens!" clucked the chickens as they saw the head guard dog, Muxtar, passing by.

"Hurrah!" barked Muxtar.

"We demand that enemies of the coop be punished!" fretted the chickens. "Peck, peck, peck all foes of the coop!"

"The enemies will be punished and pecked," promised Muxtar. "Polkan and I are headed to the Far Woods right now to apprehend the enemies and bring them back here!"

"All hail Polkan!" squawked the chickens. "Veteran Polkan!"

"Hello, friends!" Polkan, an elderly hunting hound, made his way out of his doghouse at the far end of the yard and jogged, limping, towards the coop. His right ear was torn and his fur was graying. Three gold medals jangled on his chest: for courageous hunting, committed hunting, and callous hunting.

"Hail to the coop! Hail to the hens! And the eggs! And Muxtar! And Polkan! All hail the coop!" the chickens sang shrilly.

"Let's pick up the pace," whispered Muxtar, and they sped up in the direction of the Far Woods.

"My ears are still ringing from their squalling," complained Polkan. "How do you stand it all day long? At least my doghouse is far away, but yours is right next to the coop…"

"Oh, I've gotten used to it. I just do my job and try not to pay their clucking any attention. I bark a 'hurrah' at them now and then. They like that word."

"*Hurrrrah*," Polkan drew out dreamily. "It *is* a great word. I remember my first Hunt—I was scared. There I was, gearing up to attack for the first time in my life and I needed some encouragement, so I barked out a deafening '*hurrrrah*' into the woods. And all the birds and squirrels in the trees screeched in fear. And I wasn't scared anymore. *Let everyone fear me, I'm their worst nightmare...*, I'd thought to myself."

"It's hard to believe that you were ever scared of anything," said Muxtar. "You're fearless!"

"Well, back then I was still young, just a spring chicken," said Polkan, breathing heavily.

"What? You were a chicken?"

"No—a spring chicken means someone who's young and inexperienced. We use this phrase—"

"Hurrah," interrupted Muxtar.

"What was that for?" asked Polkan, taken aback.

"You're very smart. You know lots of expressions. You're brave. Hurrah!"

"Could you slow down? I can't quite keep up," asked Polkan.

"Of course, friend."

"No, I don't deserve any hurrahs anymore," sulked Polkan. "I'm completely out of shape. An old hunting hound is a bad hunting hound."

"Who says?" asked Muxtar, indignant.

"Nina Palna."

"Oh. Then it's a fact," said Muxtar.

"Nina Palna plans on getting a new hunting hound. To replace me."

Muxtar didn't respond.

"Once upon a time I was awarded medals for courage, commitment, and callousness," said Polkan. "And Nina Palna praised my Jaws of Death."

"Don't worry, friend. We'll bring the fox and kittyraccoon back to Huntington Farm and you can committedly tail them, courageously chase them, and callously maul them in our yard—just like you would in a Hunt."

"In the yard...," said Polkan, more dejected than ever. "Why are you so sure we'll bring the fox and kittyraccoon back? What if they won't turn over their own?"

"Don't worry. The police badger will hand them over, alright. I looked into his eyes and saw right through him—he's a coward. He really doesn't want a Hunt. So don't worry. The fox and kittyraccoon are as good as ours. Yeah?"

"Yeah," nodded Polkan uncertainly. "But, you know, it's a bit unfair. To hunt them in the yard. There's nowhere to hide, nowhere to run—not like in the woods. It's not a fair fight."

"Why do you care? The point is to maul them..."

"*Shh*," whispered Polkan, standing at attention. "I sense them. The badger and the cat. And our chicken."

"But we aren't in the woods yet," said Muxtar surprised. "The woods don't start until way over there, on the other bank of the brook..."

"I sense them," said Polkan stubbornly. "My sense of smell hasn't left me yet."

"Can you smell their fear?"

"The kittyraccoon is a bit scared, yes. The chicken is terrified. But the badger isn't."

"Wait—the chicken is alive?"

"She smells alive and well."

"What about the fox? Is she very scared?"

"There isn't a fox with them. Instead there's..."

"What do you mean, there isn't a fox?!"

CHAPTER 4: IN WHICH SCARS DECORATE AN ANIMAL

"Wherrrre's the felonious fox?" barked Muxtar in place of a greeting. "I *orrrrdered* you to hand *overrrr* the ferretcat and fox for mauling! I see the ferretcat, but not the fox. How dare you disobey my *orrrrders!*"

"First off, you don't see a ferretcat," said Chief Badger calmly. "This is Badgercat–Assistant Badger of the Far Woods Police. There aren't any ferretcats in the Far Woods. Second off, I'd advise you to calm down and get a hold of yourself–you're foaming at the mouth. Third off–"

"For the record!" shrieked Chicken Four.

"Wait," Badgercat cut her off.

"Third off, the police of the Far Woods aren't subject to your orders," continued Badger. "The chicken, Badgercat, and I have come here for peace talks. The chicken has something to say too."

"Peace talks?" Muxtar hurriedly wiped the foam from his snout, but his anger caused a new batch to start forming immediately. "She has something to say too? Either return the chicken or–"

"For the record!" the chicken piped up.

"Zip it, fool!" snarled Muxtar. "Either return the fool–I mean fowl–along with the others for mauling or there'll be a Hunt, lead by the great hunting hound Polkan," he nodded in Polkan's direction. "I expect the animals of the Far Woods still remember his Jaws of Death."

"Yes, we do," said Badger respectfully. "That's exactly why we brought along a veteran of the last Woodland Hunt."

"I thought I smelled an old acquaintance," sniffed Polkan, baring his teeth. "Yes, an old, fur-bearing animal..."

An elderly ferret came out of the bushes into the clearing. Though he limped, he walked with dignity. His chest was adorned with medals for beastly valor.

"Hello to you, ruthless Polkan," said Ferret.

"And hello to you, fearless Ferret," answered Polkan.

"I remember your famous Jaws of Death well," said Ferret. "I remember how you clamped down on my back left paw—it still aches when the weather changes."

"And I remember how you bit into my ear in return," Polkan smirked. "It never did heal."

"We don't need a repeat of that horrible Hunt, don't you agree?" Ferret narrowed his red eyes.

"I agree," said Polkan. "Even more reason for the Far Woods to comply with our wishes—return the chicken and those guilty of her theft and there won't be a Hunt."

"You see," said Badger, "it's impossible for us to comply with your wishes—because there was no theft. And, so, no guilty animals."

"What do you mean, 'there was no theft'?" gaped Muxtar. "What about the chicken?"

"The chicken," said Badgercat, elbowing the chicken discreetly, "has something to say on this matter."

"For the record," Chicken Four perked up. "I left the coop and went to the Far Woods with my friend Fox voluntarily. No one forced me to do so."

"Since when are our chickens friends with foxes?" Polkan raised his furry eyebrows. "And leave the comfort of the coop for the wilderness of the woods?"

"Well, um...," stammered Chicken Four. "The thing is..."

"Tell them why," Badgercat whispered in her ear. "Tell them why you don't want to go back to Huntington Farm."

"I don't want to go back to Hunting Farm!" squawked Chicken Four. "I'll be eaten! Nina Palna will make soup out of me! And give my b-b-b-bones to the dogs! I left the coop and went to the Far Woods with my friend Fox voluntarily. No one forced me to do so! No one forced me to do so!"

"You can see for yourselves, dear dogs: there was no theft," Chief Badger spread his paws. "And since there was no theft—there aren't any perpetrators."

"*Alrrrright*," growled Muxtar. "But we're taking the chicken."

"Okay," shrugged Badger. "If she's willing to go with you."

"She doesn't have a choice. She belongs to Huntington Farm."

"Currently, you are on the territory of the Far Woods," said Badgercat proudly. "Which means *our* laws are in effect. According to the laws of the

Far Woods, all animals and birds are free beings and have the right to decide where and how to live."

"I'll show you a free being, kittyhamster!" Muxtar came right up to Badgercat, baring his teeth—they were as sharp and crooked as the spikes on a rickety farm fence. "You reek of a stray cat. I hate strays..."

Muxtar's breath smelled of death and indigestion. Badgercat shut his eyes and flattened his ears against his head.

"...I have an instinct," Muxtar licked his lips. "As soon as I see a stray cat—I attack." Muxtar opened wide and chomped the air an inch away from Badgercat's neck with his spiky teeth. Badgercat barely had time to leap out of the way.

"Are you boys fighting over me?" asked Chicken Four dreamily.

Muxtar emitted a deep growl.

"Down!" yelled Chief Badger. "Everyone calm down! Stand down!"

Muxtar began growling again. Badgercat hissed threateningly in reply.

"What a brave boy!" Ferret's red eyes filled with giant tears.

Badgercat arched his back, puffing up his fur in order to look as big as possible.

But I'll never be as big as this nasty mutt, thought Badgercat, letting out his claws to their maximum length. *Thing's aren't looking good. It's not an even fight. These two—a guard dog and hunting hound will easily maul all three of us. Ferret's an invalid, Badger's out of shape, and I can't take on two rabid dogs on my own, even though I'm superagile and quick—*

But Badgercat didn't have time to finish his thought: Muxtar's teeth chomped down again and again and then, everything went black because Badgercat's head ended up in Muxtar's jaws.

Darkness, a horrible stench, and increasing pain overtook Badgercat—he felt the dog's jaws slowly but relentlessly closing around his throat. He swatted blindly at the dog's snout with his claws. Muxtar wailed but didn't let go. From the outside world Badgercat could hear muted, barely recognizable sounds, as if coming from some faraway world. The chicken's clucking, Ferret's indistinct yelps, Badger's helpless, desperate voice:

"Drop it!"

"Let him go!"

"You're attacking a police officer!"

Muxtar didn't let go. Instead his jaws squeezed ever tighter.

Any minute now I'll hear a crunch—he'll snap my neck in two, thought Badgercat. *What a disgraceful way for a young and agile police officer to die–in the jaws of a farm guard dog...*

Any minute now, I'll snap his neck in two, thought Muxtar. *This obnoxious kittyhamster deserves a disgraceful death...*

"Let him go," Polkan suddenly spoke up. "Let the police officer go, friend."

"*Bot my inshtincsh,*" mumbled Muxtar, his jaw clamped tight.

"It's good to have passionate instincts," said Polkan. "But you've got to be stronger than your passions. Let the gophercat go."

Muxtar thought for a second, then spit Badgercat out.

"I'm not a gophercat," mumbled Badgercat, plopping onto the ground. "I'm Assistant Chief Badger of the Far Woods Police. Do you know the punishment for attacking a police officer?"

"Count your blessings that you're alive, Assistant Chief Gopher," smirked Polkan. "Let's go, Muxtar. We're done here. Let the chicken stay with them."

"Let the chicken stay?" Muxtar cocked his head, trying to detect some additional secret meaning to Polkan's words.

"Yes," Polkan nodded calmly. "Because she's a traitor. This chicken betrayed her coop. She ran away, leaving her sisters in harm's way. We don't need traitors at Huntington Farm. Let's go." And the dogs jogged silently in the direction of the brook.

"I'm not a traitor," whispered Chicken Four.

"Thank goodness that's over," smiled Ferret.

"Son, are you hurt?" Chief Badger leaned over Badgercat. "Let me have a look."

"I'm not a traitor," repeated Chicken Four. "I love my coop and my sister hens."

"It's okay. The bite isn't too deep." Badgercat stood up, shaking himself off. "But I think it'll leave a scar."

"Scars decorate an animal," said Ferret.

"I'm not a traitor. I've got to go back to my coop."

"What are you clucking about?" frowned Badger. "You know what'll happen if you go back. They'll eat you."

"I have to do everything I can," insisted the chicken. "I have to warn my friends about the danger. Tell them what really happens in Nina Palna's kitchen on Fridays."

"But...that's suicide!"

"Not suicide—a heroic deed!" declared Chicken Four. "We chickens are the proudest breed and spread our wings in awe, to celebrate heroic deeds we proudly cluck hurrah! Thank you for your help, woodland

friends. I'll lay you an egg to remember me by." And she immediately laid an egg. "Now I've got to go."

The chicken began running after the two giant dogs, wildly flapping her wings and singing loudly: "O'er mountains and meadows may we chickens keep soaring! And as we vanquish our foes, 'all hail the coop' we'll keep crowing!"

"Does she think she's flying?" asked Badgercat looking after her.

Ferret nodded. "But at least there's room for heroic deeds in her life," he said.

"I feel sorry for that foolish bird," said Badger sadly. "She'll be slaughtered. But look at this beautiful egg she laid for us."

The three of them mournfully gazed at the egg—snow-white and still warm.

"I guess we probably ought to save her," said Badgercat tentatively. "What should we do?"

"Personally, I'm going into hibernation," Badger rubbed the bridge of his nose sleepily. "You can't save someone who doesn't want to be saved, Son. We offered the chicken a safe place here in the Far Woods, but she left. It was her choice. We did everything we could."

"But I'm sure we could do more," insisted Badgercat.

"We absolutely must do something," Ferret straightened out his hunched back with effort. "It's our duty to help our chickens."

"They aren't our chickens—they're farm chickens," corrected Badger.

"Whatever," Ferret waved him off. "We've got to help our feathered sisters."

"I don't have any feathered sisters," protested Badgercat.

"He's talking about the chickens," explained Badger.

"I don't have any chicken sisters either."

"I mean that all animals are brothers and sisters. And we've got to help one another."

"Agreed! We've got to help," Badgercat finally understood.

Sleep, thought Badger. *How I'd love to go to sleep. It's getting colder and colder, and it smells of winter. The frost on the fallen leaves looks just like white feathers. Winter is almost here. Why do we have to help those farm birds? Why should I care about the chickens when it's almost winter and I have a heated floor waiting for me? It's not my responsibility... And I'm so very tired. I have the right to sleep. Let the chickens sing heroic anthems, let Nina Palna make soup out of them... I'll be asleep...*

But out loud he said, "What, exactly, are you suggesting?"

"Well, we could take Wolf, Fox, the coyote, and a dozen other guys to Huntington Farm and just free all the chickens," suggested Ferret.

"And then do what with them?" asked Badger.

"I don't know. Bring them here to the Far Woods. They could lay eggs for us."

"And what are we going to do with the eggs?"

"What do you mean? We'll eat them!"

"Well, eggs are future chickens. That's to say they're young chickens. And, according to the laws of the Far Woods, eating animals—of any age—is illegal. We don't eat nightingale or partridge eggs."

"*Hmm*. So then they're useless," Ferret thought for a minute. "Then just let them live here, proliferate."

"And you think Nina Palna will like that her chickens are proliferating in our woods? Or do you think she'll want them back and send hunting hounds along with hunters and rifles to deal with us?"

"The latter," sulked Ferret.

"I have a different idea," perked up Badgercat. "We could ask Wolf to help with Nina Palna...you know... take her out of the equation."

"Take her out of the equation?" asked Badger, looking for clarification.

"Well, you know, Nina Palna isn't an animal—and our laws say it's illegal to eat animals, which means when it comes to nonanimals..."

"Badgercat. You are a police officer. Are you seriously suggesting that Wolf eat Nina Palna?"

Badger's whiskers stood on end. "Or am I just hearing things?"

"You're just hearing things," grumbled Badgercat.

"That's what I thought," said Badger, nodding.

"If you don't like any of our ideas, then let's hear yours," griped Ferret.

"My idea is that we make a pact with Nina Palna—that she won't eat chickens anymore."

"And why would she agree to that?" asked Badgercat.

"That, my friend," said Badger, smoothing out his whiskers, "is the crux of the matter: how to convince Nina Palna. For starters we've got to find out two things: what Nina Palna loves most of all and what she's most afraid of."

"How're we going to do that?"

"By putting the life of a member of the police at risk," said Badger seriously. "But I think he'll manage. He's very capable."

"I'll manage," said Badgercat, turning a deep red under his fur.

"What?" asked Badger, surprised. "I wasn't talking about you."

CHAPTER 5: IN WHICH THERE'S A MURDER

A dense darkness had fallen over Hunting Farm, swallowing up the pink feathered clouds and the patchy wisps of fog that hadn't made it to the horizon in time. The stars, cold and alert, like the eyes of nocturnal predators, already shone in the night sky when Chicken Four had finally reached her coop. Before entering, she looked around just to be safe—the whole way home the chicken felt like she was being followed by a wild animal, and she really didn't want to lead it straight to her coop. But the coast seemed clear. She ruffled her chilled feathers and stepped into the coop.

All the hens were fast asleep. Their husband, Brewster, was dozing on his roost. Those unsuspecting, naïve birds. Oblivious to what happens to them on Fridays in the kitchen.

"Hey, ladies!" squawked Chicken Four. "Brewster! There's been fowl play!"

"Fowl play? Where?" The chickens woke up.

A sleepy, grumpy growling came from Muxtar's doghouse nearby.

"Fowl play? How? Where? Fowl play? Who? Why?" trilled the chickens.

"Something's a *fowwwwl*," crowed Brewster. "But what exactly?" he clarified, a bit calmer.

"It's Nina Palna," sobbed Chicken Four. "She doesn't love us. In fact, on Fridays...in her kitchen... she makes...chicken soup!"

"Chicken soup!" crowed Brewster outraged. "On Fridays she makes chicken soup!"

"Chicken soup! Chicken soup, chicken soup, chicken soup!" echoed the chickens.

"Freedom to our coop!" crowed Brewster. "We're not soup!"

"Notsoup, notsoup, notsoup!" the chickens were getting nervous. "Freedom! The Coop is anti-soup!"

"The coop is anti-soup!" Brewster proudly spread his wings. "Stop the soup!"

"Stop the soup! Stop the soup! Stop the soup!" clucked the chickens.

"Stop the soup!" Chicken Four chanted along with them. "Stop the soup! Stop the soup..." She froze, her beak wide open.

A huge shadow loomed over her. The shadow smelled of death. The shadow had shallow, heavy breathing. Chicken Four watched in silence as the swaying black form slowly took on its predatory shape and opened its fanged mouth.

"Danger!" the chickens clucked hysterically.

"Danger," silently mouthed Chicken Four.

She slowly turned to face the source of the shadow. She wanted to see the face of her murderer. And before that initial squirt of blood, like the juice from a popped cranberry, before she was overtaken by complete and total darkness, before the clucks had gone mute, she had time to think, *But I thought we were girlfriends now...*

And then the predatory jaws clamped down on the helpless chicken's neck.

"Murder!" the chickens began running around horrified. "Murder! Murder! Murder!"

"Fox in the coop!" crowed Brewster desperately.

CHAPTER 6: IN WHICH EVERYONE FEELS VERY SORRY FOR THE BIRD

"**R**emember, you're a chick now," said Chief Badger. "Under no circumstances are you to take off this costume while you're at Huntington Farm."

Starling jumped in place a few times and nodded. He liked the fluffy yellow chick costume. It had holes for his eyes, beak, and feet. Inside the costume, it was warm and cozy, like inside of a nest. Why would he ever want to take it off?

"Try not to arouse any suspicion," continued Badger. "It'll be easy for you. Just repeat everything the chickens say and they'll think you're one of them.

41

They're too stupid to tell the difference between a chick and a starling."

"They're too stupid," repeated Starling.

"Your mission is to infiltrate the coop under the guise of a chick and gather information about Nina Palna. This is called 'working undercover.' Okay?"

"Working undercover. Okay."

"We want to know what Nina Palna loves most of all and what she's most afraid of."

"What Nina Palna loves most of all and what she's most afraid of," echoed Starling.

"We also need information about the murder of the chicken. You've got to carefully question the witnesses. But don't blow your cover."

"Carefully question the witnesses," said Starling.

"As soon as you've gathered the information, return to the Far Woods," said Chief Badger, patting Starling on the head. "Take care of yourself."

"Good luck at Huntington Farm, Starling!" said Badgercat.

"Happy to be of service to the Far Woods Police," said Starling brightly.

"All right, it's time," said Badger, his whiskers twitching nervously. "Off you go."

"Off I go," squeaked Starling and soared off into the sunrise.

"Since when can he speak for himself?" asked Badgercat, watching the yellow blob in the sky. "'Off I go,' and 'I'm happy to serve.'"

"Not sure," said Badger. He, too, was looking after the yellow ball of fluff, which had now become a tiny black dot. "He must've heard it somewhere."

"He sure is talented," nodded Badgercat.

"*Rrrrruuuuuffffff!*" Suddenly came a now familiar enraged bark.

A second later Muxtar emerged from the bushes. His tongue hung out of his mouth, trembling and dried out from his brisk run, his scruff was standing on end, his nose was wrinkled menacingly, and his furry chin was covered in burrs.

"You woodland animals really are beastly!" he roared.

"How so?" Chief Badger stared at Muxtar blankly.

"How-how-how—" Muxtar stammered furiously. "How so? Your fox murdered our chicken after all!"

"Chicken Four?" whispered Badgercat.

"Fox? Impossible!" said Chief Badger.

"It's possible all right," snarled Muxtar. "The other chickens witnessed the murder. And each and every last one of them confirm that the murderer was a fox. The rooster confirmed it too. Hand over the fox immediately!"

"Bring in Fox for questioning, and snap to it," Badger ordered Badgercat. "I'm sure there's been some mistake."

"I can't bring her in," admitted Badgercat. "I haven't seen her since yesterday, when Doc Hawk was reviving the chicken. Afterward, Hawk looked all over the woods for Fox. He wanted to prescribe her some calming berries to help combat her aggression and predatory instincts, but she was nowhere to be found. Not in her den, not in the thicket, not in the clearing–nowhere. Apparently, she was last seen at the Tree Knot Tavern. She drank three mothitos and ran off without paying."

"Holy claw!" yelped Badger.

"I'd say," growled Muxtar. "Now I see that you have absolutely no control over your fellow animals, Chief Badger. I'm declaring a Hunt on the Far Woods."

"Wait, is she...I mean the chicken...is she definitely dead?" asked Badgercat, a bit hopeful. "Maybe she was just slightly strangled, like last time? You know, chickens are very resilient–"

"The chicken is definitely dead," interrupted Muxtar. "We have the body. And footage from a security camera. I've brought it here as evidence."

"Poor bird!" sputtered Badgercat. "She laid an egg for us. We shouldn't have let her go…"

"Footage," said Badger, concerned. "We have a bit of a problem. The thing is, it's very hard to connect modern farm technologies to our Far Woods' root tube system. Our specialist, electric Ray, can probably figure it out, but it'll take him some time—a month and a half or two, at least. Is the footage on a tape, a disk, or a flash drive?"

"I don't know any of those words," said Muxtar, catching himself cocking his head reflexively to one side, trying to understand what was being said. "You, Badger, must think of yourself as mighty smart." He shook himself off. "Don't try to confuse me with your fancy words. I just ripped the security camera off the tree, bit through the cables, and dragged it here. It wasn't light either. I left it there, in the bushes."

"Oh good," sighed Badger, relieved. "Since there's a piece of cable, Ray can connect it to the roots in no time and we can watch the footage on the root tube at the station."

CHAPTER 7: IN WHICH UNDERCOVER WORK BECOMES DANGEROUS

"Look, darling," said Pence. "There's a starling wearing a chick costume flying overhead."

Petunia looked up at the sky with difficulty. Unlike her husband, who was a rather trim and sporty miniature pig, she was a large, portly hog whose stiff neck was swimming in fat.

"It's true, my dear," she said. "A sign of rain, I reckon. The sky looks foreboding."

"I don't mind rain. What I worry about is getting slaughtered."

"You're right, dear," sighed Petunia. "It's a dog eat dog world."

"You've got to lose weight my darling," said Pence anxiously. "You're gloriously obese, but better to sacrifice your beauty than be slaughtered and eaten. You know what Nina Palna does to the fattest, most beautiful pigs—she stuffs them with nuts, apples, and honey, and roasts them. I won't survive if that happens to you. I'd rather love the skinny version of you."

"I'm trying, dear, but I haven't been able to conquer my natural beauty just yet," Petunia nuzzled up to her husband with her whole body, almost knocking him over. "We've got to cherish every moment we have together. Apart from Nina Palna, now there's a killer fox roaming Huntington Farm!" The pig switched to a whisper. "And, by all accounts, this fox is a real maniac. She murdered a chicken last night for no reason at all. She didn't even eat it—just left it in the yard!"

"There's something you don't know about the murder. What I mean is—you only know what you've heard from the chickens and dogs. But you didn't see anything for yourself because you sleep so soundly, darling, just like a newborn. You sleep so well because your soul is innocent and pure. And you snore so sweetly, just like—"

"Weren't you asleep too?" Petunia was so surprised she didn't even let her husband finish complimenting her. "You saw what happened in the coop?"

"I haven't been sleeping well, darling. I keep thinking about your extra weight and the apple-nut-honey stuffing... So, yes, I saw something. Something very strange."

And he proceeded to tell his wife everything he saw.

"It's a dog eat dog world!" squealed Petunia after he finished. "You can't trust a soul."

"Oh, look, darling, the starling wearing a chick costume flew right into the coop."

"That poor bird! They'll peck him to death—they don't like wild birds."

"They won't. They're too stupid. They'll think he's a real chick."

Petunia followed the starling with her beady eyes. Pence loved looking into them on sunny days—the sunrays made them sparkle like tiny gemstones.

"Hey, Pence. You don't think that starling is a spy, do you? Why is he flying into the coop dressed as a chick anyway?"

* * *

Starling was indeed worried that the chickens would sense an intruder and immediately peck him to death. But when he flew into the coop, Brewster, the hens, and the chicks were all chanting "stop the soup," "chicken murder," and "chicken slaughter," and Starling joined the chorus and no one noticed a thing.

"Chickens are murdered!" crowed Brewster once more.

"Chickens are slaughtered!" clucked his wives and children.

"Who murders chickens? Murders chickens? Murders chickens?" asked Brewster. "Who slaughters chickens? Slaughters chickens? Slaughters chickens?"

"Fox murders chickens! Nina Palna slaughters chickens!"

"The terrible Fox!" sang Brewster. "The maniacal Fox!"

"Fox isn't a friend!" one chicken's voice suddenly stood out from the chorus. "Fox's face is motionless! Fox's grimace is terrifying!"

Starling gaped at the screaming chicken. She looked exactly like all the others. The starling didn't have a knack for remembering faces, so all the chickens in the coop looked identical to him. He did, however, have quite a knack for remembering voices—and he would've recognized this voice out of a million others. It was Chicken Four. The same one who ate all his nuts at the police station. The same one who'd apparently been murdered by Fox.

"Fox's face is motionless?" repeated Starling in the chicken's voice, but with the intonation of a question.

Actually, Starling was capable of speaking for himself, he just didn't do it very often. Because his grandfather, Starling the Elder, once explained to him (and these words were permanently etched in his memory) that there was no better way to find something out from an animal than to repeat their words back to them. That way, the animal thinks they're talking to themselves, and animals trust themselves wholeheartedly. So eventually the animal ends up spilling all their secrets. The main thing was to calmly and accurately repeat their key words.

"Fox's face was absolutely motionless!" confirmed Chicken Four. "It was terrifying to see the stone face of a murderer!"

"Fox's grimace is terrifying?" clarified Starling in the chicken's voice.

"Yes, terrifying! More so than the first time, when Fox dragged me to the Far Woods. That time I didn't even understand what had happened. But last night...I was sure my hour had come," Chicken Four burst into tears. "When I looked into the murderer's immobile eyes, I fainted!"

"My hour had come," repeated Starling, adding a sob, just in case.

"Oh yes! Our poor, poor Chicken Five! Last night her hour had come! She was murdered by a monster! She was murdered by the crazed Fox."

"Chicken slaughter! Chicken slaughter!" clucked the others. "Chicken murder! Chicken murder!"

"Nina Palna slaughters chickens!" said Starling. He wanted to lead the conversation toward what he needed to find out: what Nina Palna was afraid of and what she loved. "Nina Palna murders chickens!"

All the chickens suddenly fell silent. They stared at Starling, their eyes narrowed in suspicion. Starling realized his mistake—he hadn't repeated their words exactly—but it was too late. Evidently, the chickens had never said that Nina Palna murdered chickens, only that she slaughtered chickens.

"What what?" Brewster hopped off his roost and made his way to Starling, his comb shaking. "What what, what what, what what? Nina Palna doesn't murder chickens!"

"Doesn't murder! Doesn't murder! Doesn't murder!"

"She butchers chickens!" he declared, coming right up to Starling.

"Butchers! Butchers! Butchers!"

Brewster stuck out his neck and roughly plucked at Starling's wing with his beak. The chick costume split at the seam and the fluffy yellow fabric hung off to one side, revealing Starling's dark brown feathers.

"*Fowwwwl plaaaaay!*" cackled Brewster. He grabbed Starling with his scaly, yellow claw. "*Intruuuuder* in the *coooooop!*"

"Starling...," said Chicken Four, stunned. "Brewster, it's Starling. He isn't an intruder. He's from the Far Woods. I know him."

"There's a starling in the *coooooop!*" Brewster crowed shrilly. "A killer starling from the Far *Woooooods*! Muxtar! Polkan!"

"They aren't here, Mr. Brewster," came a squeaky yap from the doghouse. "They went to the Far Woods."

"We're under attack, and they're in the Far Woods?" Brewster was indignant. "By the way, who are you?"

"I'm the new dog," a puppy came out of the dog-house and shook himself off. "I'm a purebred hunting hound." The puppy had long ears and disproportionately large paws.

"Are you the new Polkan? But you're just a small fry!"

"I'm not a small fry. I'm a puppy," growled the puppy. "My name's Count. When I grow up, I'll take Polkan's place. Nina Palna got me specifically to replace him. Polkan's too old. He isn't a good hunter anymore. He's out of shape. But I'm a superbreed of hunting hound. I'm even pedigreed! I'm good for hunting wolves and foxes and any other animals—"

"Well, since you're such a hunter, why don't you catch this killer starling," Brewster shook the starling clutched in his claw. "Before he murders all of us."

"He's not a killer," protested Chicken Four. "I know him. He's harmless!"

"Is he as harmless as your friend Fox?" glared Brewster.

"I think she's right," said Count, cocking his head to the side and examining Starling. "He really doesn't look like a killer."

"You're not supposed to think. You're supposed to chase and retrieve," scolded Brewster. "That is, if you are indeed a hunting hound and not just a lap dog."

"A lap dog? I'll show you!" Count lunged awkwardly toward Brewster, grabbed the starling in his teeth, and bolted toward the house.

"She'll probably make soup out of him," whispered Chicken Four.

"Good. We've got to defeat our foes," said Brewster. "The last thing we need is all sorts of filthy woodland birds milling about without punishment."

"Defeat! Defeat!" the other chickens started up. "Punishment! Punishment!"

CHAPTER 8: IN WHICH A HUNT IS DECLARED ON THE FAR WOODS

A group of animals huddled around the security camera, watching the footage. The dim, blurred silhouette of an animal in the dark. Its face isn't visible. It carefully creeps toward the coop, crouched low to the ground, its head lowered, trying to blend in with the grass and its own shadow. It's trying to be invisible, moving swiftly yet smoothly. The mannerisms of a predator. The mannerisms of a professional murderer.

Right at the chicken coop it freezes. It carefully chooses its target. It crouches low and lifts a front paw, a barely noticeable movement. The stance of a predator ready to pounce; of a predator in anticipation of tasting blood. Then, it tilts its beastly snout toward the full moon—and toward the hidden camera, so that finally, if only the slightest bit, its face can be made out.

Chief Badger was very familiar with this dreamy look toward the moon before the lightning-fast ambush—a short, mysterious ritual, performed by predators at night. Having chased many criminals, Badger had seen this ritual performed more than once. But why the moon? It was as if they were asking it for permission to kill. Maybe they believed that the cunning, bloodthirsty god of predators lived on the moon. Of course, Badger knew that no one lived on the moon and that the moon was actually just a wheel of cheese that the Evil Owl Spirit slowly ate away at all month long, only to be created anew by the Good Woodland Spirit. However, criminals, on the whole, were uneducated, superstitious creatures and were quite capable of believing all sorts of nonsense. Thus continuing to pray to a nonexistent predator god before every attack, staring into the night sky with their motionless, unblinking eyes...yes, strangely motionless...completely unblinking...

"Can you pause, Ray?" asked Chief Badger, and the predator obediently froze on the screen of the root tube.

"Why'd you stop it?" growled Muxtar. "You're wasting time!"

"Ray, can you zoom in on the face of the assailant?" said Badger, ignoring Muxtar. "Yes, that's good...and a bit more...Now Vulture, look at the face closely. You're the expert here."

"Very strange," Vulture nodded cryptically. "Quite odd indeed..."

"It's obviously a fox," said Muxtar growing annoyed. "What's the point of zooming in? And what's so strange?"

"Yes, it's a fox all right," mumbled Badger. "But is it our Fox?"

"Whose else's could she be?" Muxtar cocked his head to one side.

"Maybe she's a stray from the Near Woods?" suggested Badgercat.

"Or a farm fox," said Chief Badger.

"A farm fox?" Muxtar cocked his head to the other side. "We don't have any foxes at Huntington Farm!"

"Regardless, the quality of the image is very poor," said electric Ray.

"The quality is fine," barked Muxtar. "Don't beat around the bush, electric eel. Turn it back on. Your fox is about to murder our chicken."

Ray looked inquisitively at Chief Badger. He wasn't about to obey Muxtar's orders. Badger nodded silently.

The fox on the screen came back to life. It seized the chicken and bit its head off. The poor bird ran around for a bit without its head and then it was over.

"The poor thing," whimpered Badgercat. "Poor Chicken Four! She laid an egg for us!"

"Hang in there, Son." Chief Badger patted Badgercat on the back.

"If I may be so bold," said Vulture. "The quality of the image doesn't allow me to determine for certain that the victim was Chicken Four and not, for instance, Chicken Five, Six, or Seven."

"Don't try to console me," hissed Badgercat. "I'm not a baby. I know that was my favorite chicken—Chicken Four!"

"Ray, can you zoom in on the victim's body?" asked Chief Badger. "My colleague Vulture and I would like to take a closer look at the bite marks."

"Holy claw!" yowled Badgercat. "I don't want to see that!"

"I agree with the kittyhamster. There's no need," said Muxtar. "In the name of Huntington Farm, I declare a Hunt on the Far Woods."

"Hold on a minute," Badger raised his paw. "What about an investigation? What about questioning witnesses? What about forensic tests?"

"Who needs all that when it's obvious what happened?" Muxtar shook himself off, rattling his heavy collar. "Your fox snuck into our coop and mauled our chicken to death. So now it's our turn to maul you."

"I insist on a further investigation!" Chief Badger tried to sound unyielding.

"Absolutely not," said Muxtar flatly. "The Hunt is about to start. Polkan and the others are already on their way. I just came early to show you the footage and to formally declare the Hunt, so that everything is fair and square."

"Fair and square would be to give us time to evac-uate the women and children," exclaimed Badger.

"Evacu-eight?" Muxtar cocked his head.

"Evacuate. Remove from the woods."

"No way. You maul our chickens—and in case you've forgotten, they're women. So we'll maul yours. Well, I've got to go meet the pack. See you soon at the Hunt."

"Find me Rabbit, now!" said Badger to Badgercat, watching after the disappearing dog. "If he wants to make up for his previous wrongdoing, here's his chance. Tell him to give them the runaround, to double back on his tracks and throw the hunting hounds off their game. It'll win us some time. At least a bit of time."

"What good will that do?" asked Badgercat desper-ately. "We're going to lose the Hunt either way."

"Never give up, friend," said Ray, encouragingly patting Badgercat on the back, causing him to jump from the electric shock, his fur and whiskers standing on end.

"Hopefully in that time Starling will return," said Badger. "I very much hope that nothing has happened to him and he'll be back any minute. With important intelligence."

"Exactly! Never lose hope!" Ray tried to pat Badgercat again, but Badgercat jumped out of his way.

CHAPTER 9: IN WHICH IT'S A DOG EAT DOG WORLD

"What a strange chick."

Nina Palna placed the starling on her cutting board and carefully examined him. She held him down with her right hand, so he wouldn't fly away, and in her left hand she held a cleaver.

"Dark brown on one side...and his other side seems to be losing feathers..." She put her cleaver aside and tugged at the costume's torn seam. The chick costume quietly slipped off the starling falling to the floor.

"My, oh my, what's this?" Nina Palna was so surprised she loosened her grip on the starling, and he

63

immediately soared to the ceiling. "And he can fly? No, it's definitely not a chick...looks more like a starling... Where do you think you're going?"

Starling made his way to the open window but ran into something sheer and unyielding–a window screen.

"You won't be flying out of here," Nina Palna smiled contentedly. "Right, Marquise? Here, kitty kitty. Come here, sweetie. Look, Marquisey-poo, we've got a woodland visitor–a starling." Nina Palna's voice became as sweet as crystallized honey. "You can catch it! Here, kitty kitty!"

Marquise hated to be called Marquisey-poo. If it wasn't for the bird, she would've simply ignored Nina Palna. But she really wanted to catch the bird. She wanted to play with it, then smother it. So Marquise waited a few minutes, so Nina Palna would grovel a bit more, and then, her nose held high, leisurely walked into the kitchen through her custom-made cat door. There was, indeed, a starling flying around the kitchen.

"My sweetheart Marquisey-poo. How I love you, my darling kitty! If you catch the starling, I'll pluck it and cook it and you can feast on it, my sweetie."

Marquise fixed her yellow, moonlike eyes on the starling. The tip of her tail began twitching. Upon

seeing the cat, Starling panicked. He swerved sharply and flew right into a piece of twine strung with drying mushrooms that hung from the ceiling. Mushrooms rained down on the floor, on Nina Palna, and on Marquise.

"You little devil!" yelped Nina Palna. "My favorite porcini mushrooms! They're all over the floor! They're dirty! They're ruined!"

"My favorite porcini mushrooms!" yelled Starling in Nina Palna's voice. "My favorite! My favorite!"

"Yes, they're my favorite," repeated Nina Palna. "I love picking mushrooms!"

He had been right—grandfather Starling had been 100 percent right. It turns out it wasn't just animals, but people, too, who fell for his trick: repeating their words would cause them to spill all their secrets.

I might never escape this torture chamber they call a kitchen, thought Starling. *I might be plucked and cooked...but I'm a spy. I've got to complete my mission. I've got to find out what Nina Palna loves most of all and what she's most afraid of.*

"I love picking mushrooms more than anything," repeated Starling, landing on the kitchen table.

"Yes, exactly!" said Nina Palna crawling around the kitchen on all fours gathering up the mushrooms. Marquise crept up to the table and readied herself for attack.

"I love my darling kitty?" said Starling in Nina Palna's voice. "More than anything?"

"I love my darling kitty too," nodded Nina Palna. "But I love porcini mushrooms just a tiny bit more. You can fry them, roast them, marinate them, make soup out of them...But cats aren't edible. You can't cook a cat."

Marquise forgot about the starling and glared at Nina Palna in shock. She was absolutely sure that Nina Palna loved her most of all because there simply wasn't anyone or anything more perfect than Marquise herself.

Nina Palna's words insulted Marquise to her very core. Mushrooms? A fungus? Really? How could she love mushrooms more than a snow-white, fluffy, angelic cat? Nonsense! Complete and utter nonsense. Apparently, Nina Palna was in need of a reality check. Marquise crouched down, hissing, and jumped on Nina Palna's back, digging her claws into her sides.

"Help!" screeched Nina Palna causing the dishes in the china cabinet to vibrate. "Help! Wolf attack!"

Marquise gave Nina Palna's ribs a quick bite then jumped off of her onto the china cabinet and gave a satisfied stretch. *That'll show her who to love most of all*, thought the cat. She looked around in search of the starling. He was still sitting on the kitchen table, curiously studying Nina Palna's cleaver. Marquise readied herself to pounce once more...

"The big bad wolf!" Nina Palna clutched her ribs. She teetered and fell to the floor with a thud, bumping into the china cabinet on her way down. "I'm so scared! The horrible wolf!"

Marquise jumped off the china cabinet right in time, before it, too, crashed to the floor. Glasses, plates, and vases spilled out, chiming and ringing as they shattered into hundreds of fragments. Starling took flight, narrowly avoiding a careening salad bowl shard, and began circling Nina Palna like a vulture.

"I'm so scared!" he yelled in Nina Palna's voice. "The big bad wolf!"

"So that's how the cookie crumbles," said Nina Palna to herself, her eyes watering. "You live your life, not bothering a soul, and then the day comes when your very own cat suddenly turns into a wolf and attacks you. That's my biggest fear—that the story about the big bad wolf turns out to be true. And that he'll huff and puff and blow my house down and then eat me..."

She's got to be kidding, thought Marquise. *How can anyone confuse a snow-white, fluffy, angelic, supple cat with a mangy gray wolf? I'm going to catch that bird—show Nina Palna how graceful I am.* Marquise jumped onto the kitchen table, from there she grabbed on to the curtain, then leaped onto the chandelier, and finally swooped down from the swinging chandelier straight onto the starling. She overtook him midflight, backhanded him with her clawed paw, and as he fell at Nina Palna's legs, she gracefully landed nearby.

Now, I'll play with this cute little woodland bird for a bit, then smother it. And Nina Palna will make me a delicious starling soup... What's that strange sound? Sounds like hooves...

"Stop the soup!" came a chicken's shrill squawking from behind the kitchen door. And in that same instant, something heavy rammed into the door causing it to fly open.

In pranced the mini pig Pence with Chicken Four on his back. Marquise was in such shock she loosened her grip, and Starling fluttered out from under her paw.

"A pig and a chicken," identified a stunned Nina Palna. "They must want to be cooked, so they came into the kitchen."

"Free the bird!" yelped Chicken Four. "Free Starling!"

"Go on, Starling," Pence indicated toward the open door with his eyes. "Fly home!"

"Fly home?" asked Starling, fluttering above Pence.

"Yes, fly home to the Far Woods! Chicken Four told me that you were a good guy, that you—"

"Shared your nuts with me," interrupted Chicken Four.

"—shared your nuts, yes. And that you work for the Far Woods Police. Fly home and tell the Police Badgers the danger we're all in here at Huntington Farm. There are so many terrible crimes committed here. Fly fast! Chicken Four and I will cover for you. Also, there's something behind the doghouse. I think it's a piece of evidence. You've got to take it with you to the woods."

"Thank you, friends," said Starling, flying out of the kitchen. "I'll find the evidence!"

"You want Starling to do a dance?" asked Chicken Four.

"Evidence," repeated the mini pig, looking through the window after Starling, who was disappearing in the direction of the woods with the evidence in his beak. He was flying very low, as it weighed more than the bird himself. "Evidence is proof. Proof of who is guilty of—"

"Chicken slaughter!" yelped Chicken Four, not letting him finish. "Butcher! Butcher! Butcher!"

Pence tore his eyes off the window and looked up. Nina Palna was standing over him wearing her butcher's apron, the one with cherries on it. She was holding her cleaver.

* * *

"A fox mask," said Vulture. "There's no doubt about it. The piece of evidence that Starling has delivered is a fox mask."

"There's no doubt about it," said Starling and ate ten more pine nuts. "A fox mask."

"And you're absolutely sure that Chicken Four is alive?" asked Badgercat for the tenth time. "And that it was Chicken Five who was killed?"

"Absolutely sure," nodded Starling. "Chicken Four is alive. It was Chicken Five who was killed."

"Amazing news!" Badgercat began purring at a level four of bliss.

"Are you feeling better?" asked Chief Badger, watching Starling swallowing up nuts with adoration.

"Better."

"Okay. So we've got the testimonies of the chicken-witnesses. We've found out what Nina Palna loves and what she's afraid of. Now, please play the testimony of the main witness Pence the pig."

"I haven't been sleeping well, darling," said Starling in the mini pig's voice. "I keep thinking about your extra weight and the apple-nut-honey stuffing... So, yes, I saw something. Something very strange. The chicken wasn't killed by a fox. It was killed by a dog wearing a fox mask. I definitely saw that it was a dog, but I couldn't make out the breed in the dark. Darling, I think it was Muxtar. I think it bothered him that the chickens had started to rebel, chanting 'stop the soup.' I assume he killed the chicken to put an end to their uprising. But he pretended to be a fox so that Nina Palna wouldn't punish him." Starling gobbled up a few more nuts, then continued in Petunia's voice. "It's a dog eat dog world! You can't trust a soul!"

"Thank you," said Chief Badger.

"That dog, Muxtar," hissed Badgercat, letting his claws out instinctively. "I knew he couldn't be trusted."

CHAPTER 10: IN WHICH THERE'S
A RUNAROUND

Rabbit ran. Around and around he ran. He could hear the barking of the hunting hounds on his trail. The tips of his ears and tail could almost feel their hot, greedy breathing. He knew his strength was leaving him. He knew the hounds were closing in. But he kept running. He was trying to lead his pursuers as far away from the heavily populated areas of the Far Woods as possible, just like Badgercat had asked him to. Yes, he ran.

He had to make it up to the Far Woods, he had to save the animals because he had done them wrong. He had done something awful. Just recently, he had lied to and stolen from his best friend, the coyote, Yote. Just recently, he had tried to frame the innocent Wolf and take away his den. He had deceived the residents of the Far Woods and this—running in circles to the heavy beating of his own heart, throwing the hounds off their game—was the only way to win back their trust.

Circling. Circling. Doubling back on my own tracks. Leap to the right. Leap again. Then back to the left. Heartbeat. Heartbeat. Barking dogs. Wheezing dogs. The dogs are near. Heartbeat. At least there's still a heartbeat. It's deafening. Circling. Weaving. Doubling back on my own tracks. Leap to the right. Leap again. Then back... stop. I'm not the only one circling around this brook. I see someone else's tracks...someone bigger...someone more sly. They disappear under that moss-covered stump. An animal has already circled around here recently. A predator...

"What are you doing here, little Rabbit?" asked Fox unkindly. She was sitting in a hastily dug hole under the moss-covered stump. She looked menacing.

He couldn't turn back because of the dogs. But in front of him was a fox. *Well, this is the end*, he thought, freezing in place instinctively. Not that it did any good. If it had been winter and there was snow, then it would've been a different story. The white rabbit would've been invisible against the white background. Yes, in the snow he could've been still and hoped that the predator wouldn't notice him...

"What're you standing still for?" asked Fox. "You really think I can't see you against the grass and fallen leaves?"

"Are you about to maul me?" asked Rabbit point blank. He had nothing to lose. "Maul a father of twenty-five?"

"Why would I maul you?" asked Fox.

"You're a predator. A killer fox."

"And you're a stupid rabbit. Don't you get it. I'm not the one who's about to maul you. The dogs are. They'll maul you and me both."

Rabbit slowly turned around and came face to face with Polkan and Muxtar. They were breathing heavily, their tongues hanging out, their snouts pointed straight at him. Behind them was a whole pack of hunting hounds.

"If you want, we can hug," suggested Fox. "We aren't strangers, after all. They say if someone is hugging you, it's not as scary to die."

"Yes, let's hug, Fox," whispered Rabbit barely audibly.

They hugged.

"Killer Fox! You've hidden here in hopes of escaping the law. But you can't hide from us any longer! We're going to maul you and your friend Rabbit," Muxtar announced triumphantly. "Would you like to clear your dying conscience and admit to murdering the chicken?"

"I'm not a killer," sobbed Fox. "I only hid here because no one would've believed me! But I didn't do it! I didn't murder the chicken!"

"It's true. She didn't," came Chief Badger's voice. "But I know who did."

CHAPTER II: IN WHICH YOU CAN'T TRUST A SOUL

"**W**ell, well, look what the cat dragged in— suicidal woodland heroes!" snarled Muxtar looking over Chief Badger as well as Badgercat, Vulture, Starling, and the veteran Ferret who'd all arrived on his heels. "I like it when game delivers itself to the hunters. What were you mumbling about the murder?"

"I know who killed your chicken," said Badger.

"So do we. Fox," Muxtar chomped the air. "All right, Polkan," he added, turning toward him, "let's get to mauling."

"No, it wasn't Fox," said Badger calmly.

"Yes, let's go," said Polkan, nodding, and the pack of dogs collectively wrinkled their noses and began growling.

"It was a dog! A dog killed the chicken!" Badger yelled over the growling. "It was one of you! Stop the Hunt! Listen to me! I demand a cease fire!"

The growling escalated.

"You're all cowards!" Badgercat scanned the hunting hounds. "It looks like you dogs are more cowardly than our Rabbit. He wasn't scared of risking his own life to save his woods. But you're afraid of hearing the truth! Afraid to find out which dog is a liar!"

"There aren't any cowards in our pack," said Polkan proudly. "Or liars. We'll listen to the Police Badger. Then we'll resume the Hunt."

"Thank you, Polkan," nodded Chief Badger.

"Polkan is a noble hound," exhaled Fox. "I always knew that about him. Polkan respects woodland animals..."

"Enough with the flattery, Fox," frowned Polkan. "We're listening, Police Badger."

"Better yet, listen to him," said Chief Badger pointing to Starling. "This is a recording of an eye witness's testimony."

"I haven't been sleeping well, darling," said Starling in Pence's voice. "I keep thinking about your extra weight and the apple-nut-honey stuffing..."

"What kind of buffoonery is this?" barked Muxtar.

"...So, yes, I saw something. Something very strange. The chicken wasn't killed by a fox. It was killed by a dog wearing a fox mask. I definitely saw that it was a dog, but I couldn't make out the breed in the dark. Darling, I think it was Muxtar..."

"What? This is *absurrrrd*," howled Muxtar. "Don't believe him! Don't listen to him!"

A nervous growling spread through the pack. Polkan authoritatively raised his paw, ordering the dogs to quiet down.

"Continue, bird," said Polkan. "This is getting interesting."

"...I think it bothered him that the chickens had started to rebel, chanting 'stop the soup,'" continued Starling in Pence's voice. "I assume he killed the chicken to put an end to their uprising. But he pretended to be a fox so that Nina Palna wouldn't punish him..."

"He's lying!" Muxtar bared his teeth. "These are just the words of some *dirrrrty* swine! Repeated by some *dirrrrty* bird! This isn't *prrrroof*! I *swearrrrr*—"

Chief Badger looked at Muxtar, then focused on Polkan.

"Continue," said Polkan dryly.

"This theory is also corroborated by the chicken's testimony," said Chief Badger.

"Fox's face is motionless," said Starling in Chicken Four's voice. "Fox's grimace is terrifying! Fox's face is absolutely motionless! The stone face of a murderer..."

"If you take a look at our Fox," Chief Badger indicated toward Fox, who was still hugging Rabbit, "you'll see that her face is lively and animated. And that she is hardly capable of arousing such panicked fear in a victim. Look, even rabbits aren't afraid of her. Decide for yourselves."

The dogs in the pack cocked their heads to one side in unison, examining Fox and trying to decide for themselves.

"*Hearrrrsay!*" roared Muxtar. "You can't rely on the testimony of a stupid chicken!"

"But, most important, we have proof. Physical evidence," said Badger, showing the pack of dogs the fox mask. "Look. The motionless face of a fox with a terrifying grimace."

"That's not mine!" whined Muxtar. "That's not my mask. This is the first time I'm seeing it!"

"Stop it, Muxtar," said Polkan bitterly. "Stop lying to us. Aren't you ashamed of yourself? You killed one of our own, a farm chicken! And then had the nerve to give us all the runaround and blame innocent woodland animals of your crime."

"But...I didn't kill..."

"Something else that's of interest to me, are the bite marks on the victim's body," continued Badger.

"You can stop," Polkan waved him off. "There's already enough proof of Muxtar's guilt."

"If I may, I'd like to disagree," said Badger politely. "There isn't enough proof of his guilt. I actually don't think it was Muxtar who killed the chicken."

The dogs in the pack cocked their heads to one side in unison.

"What are you saying, Chief?" asked Badgercat, stunned.

"But...you said from the beginning that...," mumbled Polkan.

"I said that a dog did it."

"But the witness Pence..."

"Pence saw a dog but admitted that he couldn't make him out in the dark. Isn't that so? And he only speculated that it had been Muxtar."

"Exactly," yapped Muxtar, full of hope.

"Then who, in your opinion, killed the chicken?" asked Polkan.

"You," said Badger.

The dogs in the pack turned to stare at Polkan.

"With all due respect," said Badgercat quietly, "Chief Badger, what in the world are you talking about?"

"Yes, what in the world?" asked Polkan.

"Polkan isn't a criminal!" protested Fox. "Polkan is a kind, sympathetic dog. Unlike that one over there..." She gave Muxtar the side eye.

"So you think he's sympathetic and kind?" asked Chief Badger suddenly interested.

"Yes," said Fox.

"And how has Polkan been kind and sympathetic toward you?"

"He tried to help me. He understood my plight as a predator. He was very encouraging."

"Interesting," Chief Badger narrowed his eyes. "And how did he help and encourage you?"

"He...Polkan..." Fox hesitated. "Sometimes I'd come to roam around the coop, just to get a whiff of the chickens...since, according to the laws of the Far Woods, predators like myself must be vegetarians... but I just wanted to get a smell. So, anyway, Polkan would sometimes come out and we'd chat. He said he understood me and my predatory nature...that defying nature wasn't truly possible...that a predator would always be just that...that killing just one chicken wouldn't be a big deal...that chickens are brainless and stupid...and that they're eventually made into soup anyway..."

"Am I understanding correctly, Fox, that Polkan encouraged you to kill a farm chicken?" asked Chief Badger.

"No, no, it wasn't like that...though, maybe..." Fox faltered, wrapping herself up in her tail. "*Hmm*, it's as if he really did...did encourage me..."

"But why?" asked Rabbit.

"It's very simple actually," said Badger. "Polkan had grown old. He'd lost his famous Jaws of Death. His owner, Nina Palna, had even found his replacement—a purebred hunting puppy named... What's his name?"

"Count," said Starling.

"Yes, a puppy named Count. But Polkan couldn't come to terms with the fact that he'd been benched. He was sure that he was as strong as ever and longed to prove it to Nina Palna and win back her trust and affection. All he had to do was come up with a reason to have a Hunt. At first, Polkan just expected to goad Fox into committing the crime. To some degree his plan had worked—Fox really did attack the chicken. However, the chicken survived and even returned to the coop. So Polkan decided to stage another fox attack. He put on a fox mask and attacked the chicken himself."

"But...the coop's rebellion...Muxtar's brutal suppression of the uprising," Badgercat mumbled helplessly.

"Yes, Polkan chose the opportune time for his attack—during the uprising. He knew that if, somehow, a dog would be suspected of the crime, the suspicion would fall on the guard dog Muxtar— which is exactly what happened."

"Exactly!" barked Muxtar.

"You don't have any proof," said Polkan quietly. "I've always been on the side of peace and fairness. While Muxtar was always ferocious and hotheaded. Muxtar is the murderer."

"How dare you?" growled Muxtar. "*Frrrriends*— do you believe him?"

The dogs cocked their heads to one side in unison.

"This isn't a question of believing. There needs to be indisputable proof," said Badger wearily. "We must conduct a thorough investigation—in this case, compare bite marks. So, what do we have?" He turned to the pack of dogs, who cocked their heads in unison to the other side. "Due to Muxtar's recent attack of Assistant Chief Badger of the Far Woods Police, we have his bite marks on Assistant Chief Badger's neck. Show them the bite marks, Badgercat!"

"You see," interjected Polkan. "Muxtar has always been overly aggressive. Of course he's the murderer. And keep in mind, I was the one who played peacekeeper in the conflict between Muxtar and Gophercat…"

"We'll keep that in mind," said Badger dryly. "So we have Muxtar's bite marks on Badgercat's neck. Similarly, we have Polkan's bite marks on the body of the veteran Ferret."

"Polkan's famous Jaws of Death," the limping Ferret demonstrated his crippled hind leg. "It still aches when the weather changes—"

"Please note that Polkan's bite marks are quite distinctive: his top right fang is slightly chipped, making it all the more sharp, like a sharpened spear—"

"Oh yes, like a spear!" said Ferret. "I remember that great, that terrible Hunt—"

"So all that's left to do," interrupted Chief Badger, "is to compare Polkan's bite marks on Ferret's body and Muxtar's bite marks on Badgercat's body to the bite marks on the deceased chicken's body, and we'll know who was the murderer. We have footage from a security camera and our crime scene investigator Vulture has thoroughly examined the bite marks on the body of the victim."

"Unfortunately, due to the poor quality of the image, I cannot say for certain who the bite marks belong to," said Vulture. "The marks are very hard to see. But once zoomed in, it seems that they have the distinctive mark of a chipped fang... However, I hesitate to say so for sure."

"Slander and speculation," snarled Polkan.

"Vulture's analysis, as well as my own badger logic, lead me to believe that Polkan is the murderer," said Chief Badger. "However, Polkan is right. We do not have definitive proof of his guilt."

"Exactly," said Polkan.

"However, Vulture is willing to perform a closer examination of the victim's body. To do so, we'll

need to go to Huntington Farm," said Badger, looking at the pack of dogs. "Please grant us permission
to examine the bite marks on the body of the deceased chicken in order to establish the identity of
the murderer."

"I won't grant you anything," growled Polkan.

"And I will," growled Muxtar in response.

"I'm the alpha dog of the hunting pack," said
Polkan menacingly.

"And I'm the head guard dog. I'm about to
issue entrance permits to Huntington Farm for the
chief Badger, the kittyhamster, and the instigator
Vulture."

"And I'm about to order the pack to maul them
along with their entrance permits!"

"And you're confident they'll follow the orders of
a criminal? *Frrrriends*," Muxtar turned to the pack,
"are you going to follow the orders of a *crrrrimnal*?"

The dogs cocked their heads, thinking it over.

"We Englishmen don't follow criminal orders,"
said the English setter.

"We Russians don't either," said the Russian
wolfhound and Russian spaniel.

"The pack believes in justice," barked the
dogs in unison. "We *grrrrant* permission to enter
Huntington Farm."

"Excellent," said Chief Badger, pleased. "But we'll need an extra entrance permit," he said, turning to Muxtar.

"No problem. For whom?"

"For Wolf."

"For Wolf?" Muxtar tensed up. "Why?"

"For peace keeping purposes. Our Wolf is a famous peacekeeper. There's even stories written about him."

"All right...," said Muxtar hesitantly. "I've been known to enjoy a story or two..."

CHAPTER 12: IN WHICH DREAMS COME TRUE

"And so the bite marks on the victim's body are undeniably Polkan's," said Vulture after completing his examination. "Take a look—the distinctive mark of a spear-like broken fang."

"Poor Chicken Five," said Badgercat. "What an undeserved death!"

"Kill chickens!" Brewster was distraught. "Everyone kills chickens! And now there's a wolf in the coop!"

"Me? Never!" Wolf was offended. "I'm a famous peacekeeper! I've never killed a soul."

"We are all very sorry for your loss," said Chief Badger. "And our Wolf really is harmless. Unlike your Polkan–whom I hope will be punished to the full extent of the... Where is he anyway?"

Muxtar looked around, alarmed. Then jogged around the coop.

"He ran off, that dog!" Muxtar flattened his ears against his head in shame. "How'd I let him go? We've got to send out a search–"

"Chicken slaughter!" came a sudden shrill cry from the direction of the pigsty. "Chicken slaughter! And pig! And mini pig!"

"Chicken Four," whispered Badgercat. "I recognize her voice."

Coming from behind the pigsty fence they could hear the piercing squealing of swine, a chicken's clucking, and Nina Palna's hysterical yelps of "I'll slaughter you!", followed by "Chicken slaughter!" and "Stop the soup!" from Chicken Four. A few seconds later they all saw the mini pig Pence bounding across the yard, with Chicken Four upon his back, her wings spread majestically. Behind him, wheezing heavily, trotted his wife, Petunia. And on their heels was a beet-red Nina Palna brandishing a cleaver.

"O'er mountains and meadows may we chickens keep soaring!" sang Chicken Four, spurring on Pence.

"As we vanquish our foes, all hail the coop, we'll keep crowing!"

"I'll slaughter *yoooouuu!*" cried Nina Palna.

"Okay," said Badger, "we've come right in time. Quick. Start the chant I taught you," he said, turning to Wolf.

"I'll huff and I'll puff," howled Wolf.

Nina Palna froze, dropping her cleaver.

"I'll huff and I'll puff."

Nina Palna's eyes grew wide, and the color drained from her face.

"I'll huff and I'll puff and I'll blow your house down!"

"Wolf!" screamed Nina Palna. "Help! He'll blow my house down! He'll eat me!"

"I can help you," Chief Badger offered gallantly. "I can protect you from the wolf."

"Yes! Please help me!"

"But only under one condition. You must read and acknowledge this open letter from the residents of the Far Woods." Chief Badger handed her the letter. "They'd like to make you an offer you won't want to refuse."

Nina Palna took the letter with a trembling hand and began reading.

We, the free and wild animals of the Far Woods, would like to propose that you become a vege-

tarian and completely give up the slaughter and consumption of chickens, pigs, cows, goats, and all other farm animals. In return, we can offer you complete protection and will guarantee that the big bad wolf will, under no circumstances, blow your house down or eat you. In addition, we agree to grant you, and only you, full access to the best mushroom picking spots in the Far Woods, where no human has ever stepped foot. Every summer, we agree to alert you to the location of these spots...

"Oh my!" Nina Palna scanned the animals and winced at the sight of Wolf. "What a wonderful offer! Of course I agree to it. I've dreamed of this my whole life."

"Hail to the coop!" crowed Brewster, and all the chickens joined in. "Hail to the roosters! Hail to the eggs and the hens!"

"Hail to the Far Woods!" exclaimed Chicken Four. "Hail to the police badgers!"

"Hail to the badgers!" yelled the chickens, pigs, and dogs.

"Hail to the police badgers, of course," sounded Doc Hawk's surly voice. "But doctors shouldn't be forgotten about either. The situation was quite hopeless! I had to perform beak to muzzle resuscitation..."

"Well, well, look what the cat dragged in!" Muxtar wrinkled his nose. "Polkan!"

It was true: Polkan was trudging along the yard, staggering, his head bowed. The gray fur on his chest was matted and the three gold medals—for courageous hunting, committed hunting, and callous hunting—dragged on the ground. Doc Hawk fluttered above him, holding Polkan up by his scruff with his beak from time to time so that the dog wouldn't topple over.

"He tried to poison himself," said Hawk. "He tried to take his own life, so he ate a bunch of poisonous berries. But I couldn't let that happen. Because all animal lives are priceless! I gave him a regurgitating solution and performed beak to muzzle. The situation was quite hopeless!"

"You should've let me die in peace," growled Polkan. "Here, I'll be mauled for my crimes."

"So you admit to murdering the chicken?" asked Chief Badger.

"Yes, I do."

"What's going on?" asked Nina Palna. "Polkan killed one of my chickens?"

"Yes, I killed her," said Polkan laying down and rolling over on his back in a pose of submission. "I wanted to instigate a Hunt. I am guilty, and I'm ready for my punishment."

"I suddenly feel sorry for him," whispered Badgercat in Badger's ear.

"Then talk to Nina Palna," Badger whispered back.

"Why do you think she'll listen to me?"

"Starling said Nina Palna likes cats, so I thought..." Badger suddenly caught himself. "Err, I mean, I just thought she might like you, that's all..."

"I'm not a cat," hissed Badgercat. "I'm Assistant Chief Badger–"

"Of course, of course," nodded Badger. "It's just that sometimes you act like a cat. So Nina Palna might mistake you for a cat. That's all I meant."

"All right." Badgercat smoothed his whiskers with his paw and puffed up his tail. "I'll try."

Badgercat gracefully came up to Nina Palna, purring at a level four of bliss, and lightly brushed the tip of his tail against her leg.

"Oh, what a beautiful kitty cat!" smiled Nina Palna, leaning down to pet him. "Here, kitty kitty! What a darling. What a purring sweetie. Come here and purr into my ear," and she leaned her ear down to Badgercat.

Overcoming his disgust with difficulty, Badgercat purred into her ear.

"You really think so, darling kitty?" melted Nina Palna.

"I'm not a kitty," Badgercat couldn't stand it any longer. "I'm Assistant Chief Badger of the Far Woods Police."

"Aren't you a sweetie pie? What a little fluff ball!" said Nina Palna scratching him behind the ear.

"Holy claw!" yelped Badgercat darting away from Nina Palna, scrambling up a nearby tree.

"I've decided I won't get rid of Polkan," said Nina Palna sweetly. "I'll just take away his medals and put him on a leash for a while. Then we'll see."

"I think that's the right decision," said Badger.

"It was that fluff ball. He tugged at my heart strings. He's so sweet."

"Fluff ball?" hissed Badgercat from the tree, furiously cleaning behind his ears with his paw. "Don't even get me started—"

"Hi, fluff ball" came a gentle, sweet, though slightly mocking, voice from a nearby branch. "She calls me that too. Don't mind her."

Badgercat shuddered, puffing himself up to look as big as possible, and carefully turned around. On a nearby branch he saw a snow-white, short-haired, silk-whiskered, yellow-eyed, slender-pawed, angelic being—the most beautiful cat in the world.

"I'm Marquise," she said. "What's your name, kitty?"

"I'm not a—I'm Badgercat."

"Badgercat, Son!" came Chief Badger's voice from below. "What're you doing up there? We've solved the case. It's time to go home to the Far Woods. Let's go. Our work here is done."

"You live in the woods?" Marquise's yellow eyes grew wide.

"Yes. And unfortunately I have to say goodbye."

"But we'll see each other again, right?"

Badgercat looked at Marquise, trying to imprint her beautiful features in his memory, then jumped down without answering. What could he have said to a snow-white, angelic house cat?

"I'm not a cat," he mumbled to himself once they'd left Huntington Farm. "I am Assistant Chief Badger of the Far Woods Police."

"Of course you're not a cat," said Chief Badger, patting him on the back.

But for the first time in his life, these words didn't make him feel any better.

(To be continued...)

THE AUTHOR

Anna Starobinets is an award-winning novelist, screenwriter, and journalist who lives in Moscow, Russia. Best known as a writer of dystopian and metaphysical stories, she is also a successful children's author of fairy tales and detective stories, including four Beastly Crimes books from Dover Publications. She is the widow of the writer Alexander Garros and is raising two kids and a poodle named Cocos.

THE TRANSLATOR

Jane Bugaeva immigrated to the United States from Russia at the age of six. Forever a child at heart, she translates children's literature from Russian to English. Her translations include Anna Starobinets's *Catlantis* and the Beastly Crimes books and Sveta Dorosheva's *The Land of Stone Flowers*. Bugaeva lives in North Carolina with her husband, daughter, and two cats.